D0416732

PUFFIN BOOKS

Published by the Penguin Group
Penguin Books Ltd, 80 Strand, London WC2R 0RL, England
Penguin Putnam Inc., 375 Hudson Street, New York, New York 10014, USA
Penguin Books Australia Ltd, 250 Camberwell Road, Camberwell, Victoria 3124, Australia
Penguin Books Canada Ltd, 10 Alcorn Avenue, Toronto, Ontario, Canada M4V 3B2
Penguin Books India (P) Ltd, 11 Community Centre, Panchsheel Park, New Delhi – 110 017, India
Penguin Books (NZ) Ltd, Cnr Rosedale and Airborne Roads, Albany, Auckland, New Zealand
Penguin Books (South Africa) (Pty) Ltd, 24 Sturdee Avenue, Rosebank 2196, South Africa

Penguin Books Ltd, Registered Offices: 80 Strand, London WC2R 0RL, England

www.penguin.com

First published 2001
3 5 7 9 10 8 6 4 2

Copyright © Chris Riddell, 2001
All rights reserved

The moral right of the author/illustrator has been asserted

Set in Monotype Poliphilus

Printed at Oriental Press, Dubai, U.A.E.

Without limiting the rights under copyright reserved above, no part of this publication may be reproduced, stored in or introduced
into a retrieval system, or transmitted, in any form or by any means (electronic, mechanical, photocopying, recording or otherwise),
without the prior written permission of both the copyright owner and the above publisher of this book

British Library Cataloguing in Publication Data
A CIP catalogue record for this book is available from the British Library

ISBN 0–670–89420–6

This edition produced for The Book People Ltd, Hall Wood Avenue, Haydock, St Helens WA11 9UL

Platypus

CHRIS RIDDELL

TED SMART

"What a great day for collecting," said Platypus.

He opened his special box and took out his collection of favourite things. "Mmm . . . not bad," he said, "but I need something else."

Platypus picked up his bucket and spade and his picnic lunch. He set off for his favourite collecting place. He didn't know what else he needed, but he was sure he'd know when he saw it.

Platypus found some seaweed. "Mmm ... too slimy."

He found a rock. "Too big," he said.

He found an old shoe. "Very tempting," he said, "but I've got one already."

Platypus found lots of interesting things,
but none of them were quite right.

I wonder what time it is, he thought.

He looked in his bucket. "Lunchtime!"

After lunch, Platypus built a sandcastle.

"Mmm . . . not bad," he said. "I can take it home for my collection . . ."

. . . but he couldn't.

He picked up his bucket, and a large curly shell fell out on to his toe.

"Perfect!" said Platypus. "Just what I was looking for."

"This is what was missing from my collection," he said happily, "something to remind me of the sea."

Platypus took the curly shell home and put it in his special box. "All that collecting has made me sleepy," he said, yawning. "Time for bed."

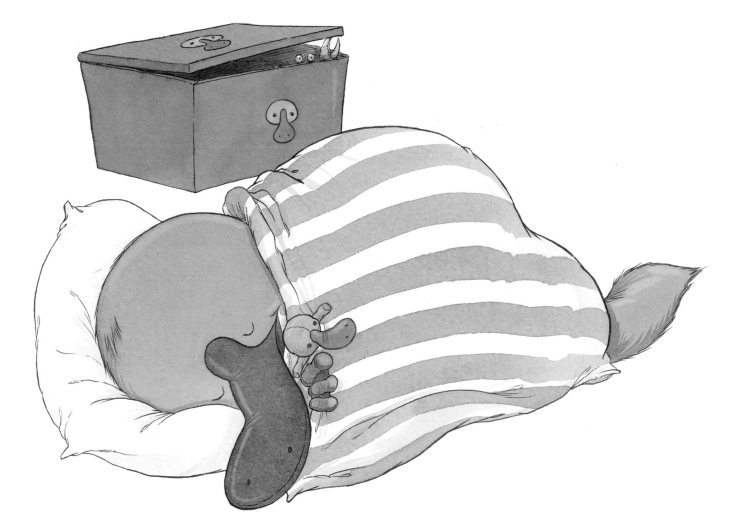

The next morning, when Platypus looked in his special box, the large curly shell had gone! He couldn't see it anywhere. "That's very strange," he said.

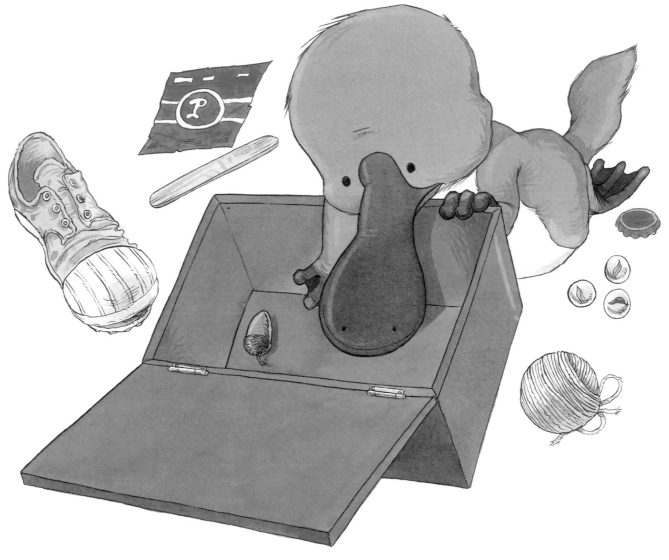

Platypus searched
everywhere for his shell.
He found an old
sandwich . . .

and a
tickling stick . . .

and another
old shoe . . .

... but no shell.

"Oh dear," sighed Platypus. "I will have to find another shell for my collection." He set off for the beach again.

On the way, Platypus saw something that looked familiar.

"That's just like my curly shell," he said.

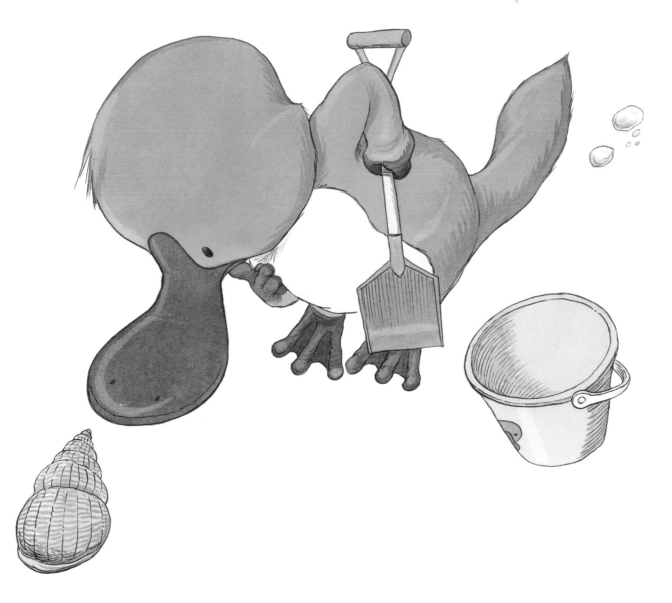

"It *is* my curly shell! How did you get here?"

He picked up the shell and ran home.

The next day, the curly shell had disappeared *again*!

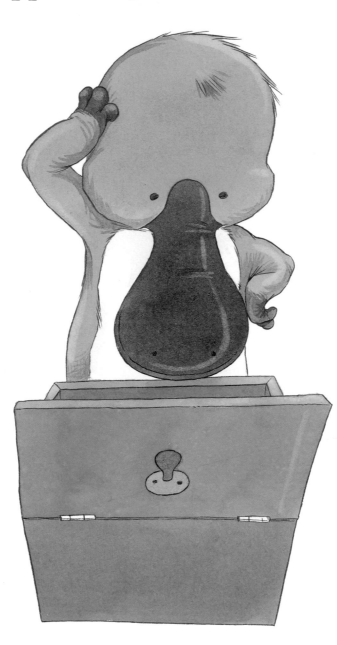

Platypus looked inside, but it wasn't there.

He looked outside, but it wasn't there either.

"Hmm," said Platypus, scratching his head. He went to his favourite thinking place and cooled his feet. He could never think with hot feet.

"Ouch!" he cried, leaping up. Something had
pinched him on the toe. It was a hermit crab
inside his curly shell!

"Oh!" said Platypus to the little crab. "I'm
sorry. If I had known the shell was your home,
I would never have collected it."

Platypus took the curly shell back to the sea in
his bucket. The hermit crab quickly scuttled off.

Platypus found a beautiful speckled shell in the sand and looked inside. It was very dark in there. "Hello, is anyone at home?" he said. There was no answer. He held the shell to his ear. He could hear the sea. "Perfect!" said Platypus.